MEL BAY PRESENTS

David Barrett's Harmoni

Scales, Patterns, & Bending Exercises #1

LEVEL 2
COMPLETE BLUES HARMONICA LESSON SERIES

CD CONTENTS

MEL BAY®

© 2000 BY MEL BAY PUBLICATIONS, INC., PACIFIC, MO 63069.
ALL RIGHTS RESERVED. INTERNATIONAL COPYRIGHT SECURED. B.M.I. MADE AND PRINTED IN U.S.A.
No part of this publication may be reproduced in whole or in part, or stored in a retrieval system, or transmitted in any form
or by any means, electronic, mechanical, photocopy, recording, or otherwise, without written permission of the publisher.

Visit us on the Web at http://www.melbay.com — E-mail us at email@melbay.com

Contents

Thanks to John Scerbo for proof reading. Also, to my wife Nozomi and our family for their never-ending support.

A Word from the Author

Welcome to *Harmonica Masterclass® Complete Blues Harmonica Lesson Series Level Two.* My name is David Barrett, the author of this lesson series. At this level you should have *Classic Chicago Blues Harp #1, Blues Harmonica Jam Tracks* and *Soloing Concepts #2,* and *Building Harmonica Technique Videos #1 and #2.* Although this book and CD combination can stand on its own, the studies found within the materials in this series will help you tremendously in understanding the ideas talked about in this book. If you have any questions regarding this book, or any other books within the line, look at the Harmonica Masterclass web-site at www.harmonicamasterclass.com or contact us by mail at P.O. Box 1723, Morgan Hill, CA 95038. Good luck and have fun!

Section 1 - **A Word About Notation**

Harmonica players use a wide variety of keyed harmonicas in their music. For ease of reading, all harmonica parts played on the ten hole diatonic harmonica will use the key signature of C major. This will put you in the pitch set of a C major harmonica. Through years of teaching, transcribing, and writing music books with Mel Bay Publications, I have found this method of notation to be the fastest for translating musical thought. Diagrammed below is a C major ten hole diatonic harmonica.

BLOW →	C	E	G	C	E	G	C	E	G	C
C	1	2	3	4	5	6	7	8	9	10
DRAW →	D	G	B	D	F	A	B	D	F	A

Harmonica Tablature

You will notice in the diagram that each hole has a corresponding number. In the tablature, the number corresponding to the hole will be under the notational symbol for the note to be played. When a number stands by itself, the note is to be drawn upon (inhaled). When a number is followed with a plus (+), the note is to be blown (exhaled). If the note is to be bent, a series of slashes will be notated to the right of the number. Each slash represents a half-step bend. For example: three draw (3), bent down a half step, would be B♭ and would be notated as 3'. Three draw, bent down a whole-step, would be A and would be notated as 3''. Three draw, bent down a whole-step and one-half (minor third bend), would be A♭ and would be notated as 3'''. Diagrammed below is the entire bend chart for a C major diatonic harmonica.

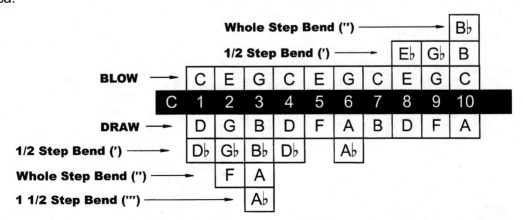

Section 2 – Diatonic Modes

When the word Diatonic is used in conjunction with a scale, it is saying that there are two half-steps and five whole-steps that the scale uses for its construction. For example, the major scale below has a half-step between the 3rd and 4th scale degree and a half-step between the 7th scale degree and octave.

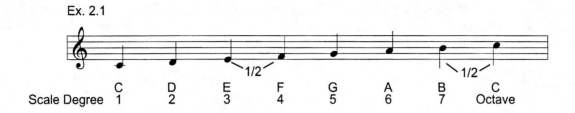

Ex. 2.1

| Scale Degree | C 1 | D 2 | E 3 | 1/2 | F 4 | G 5 | A 6 | B 7 | 1/2 | C Octave |

Changing the placement of these half-steps and whole-steps will give you different scales called modes. These modes are listed below.

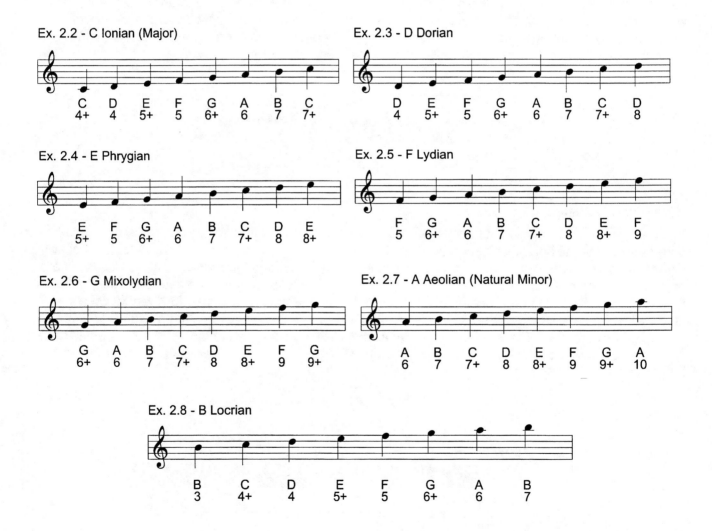

Ex. 2.2 - C Ionian (Major)

| C | D | E | F | G | A | B | C |
| 4+ | 4 | 5+ | 5 | 6+ | 6 | 7 | 7+ |

Ex. 2.3 - D Dorian

| D | E | F | G | A | B | C | D |
| 4 | 5+ | 5 | 6+ | 6 | 7 | 7+ | 8 |

Ex. 2.4 - E Phrygian

| E | F | G | A | B | C | D | E |
| 5+ | 5 | 6+ | 6 | 7 | 7+ | 8 | 8+ |

Ex. 2.5 - F Lydian

| F | G | A | B | C | D | E | F |
| 5 | 6+ | 6 | 7 | 7+ | 8 | 8+ | 9 |

Ex. 2.6 - G Mixolydian

| G | A | B | C | D | E | F | G |
| 6+ | 6 | 7 | 7+ | 8 | 8+ | 9 | 9+ |

Ex. 2.7 - A Aeolian (Natural Minor)

| A | B | C | D | E | F | G | A |
| 6 | 7 | 7+ | 8 | 8+ | 9 | 9+ | 10 |

Ex. 2.8 - B Locrian

| B | C | D | E | F | G | A | B |
| 3 | 4+ | 4 | 5+ | 5 | 6+ | 6 | 7 |

From each of these scales, chords and melodies are built. The choice of scale depends on the feel or mood of the music that you want to create. Demonstrated below are two songs that use different scales. The first example is an American folk song When the Saints Go Marching In; it uses the C major scale. The second example is a Japanese traditional song Sakura; it uses the E phrygian scale.

Section 3 – Agility Exercises

Detailed below are agility exercises that use no bends. Each exercise in this book is based on the ten hole major diatonic harmonica. Book #2 in the series will spend time on the other three tunings available from the Lee Oskar tuning system, the Natural Minor, Melody Maker, and Harmonic Minor harmonicas. All of the exercises, excluding the modes themselves, focus on patterns that will be most useful to the blues harmonica player. The most common scales in blues are those built on the notes C, G, and D (the I chord scales for 1st, 2nd and 3rd position.) Play each exercise very slowly at first, making sure that you have all of the steps. After you have mastered each pattern, speed up little by little until you can play the exercise with lightning speed.

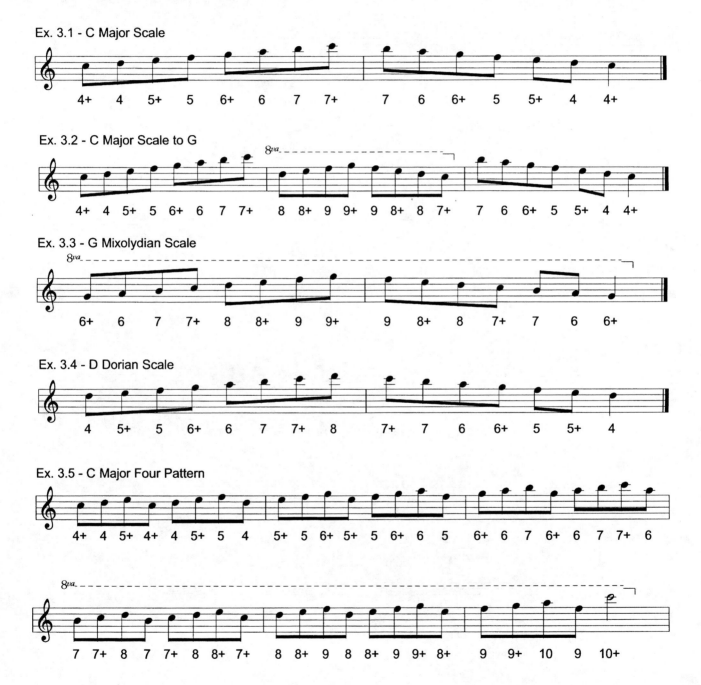

Ex. 3.1 - C Major Scale

4+ 4 5+ 5 6+ 6 7 7+   7 6 6+ 5 5+ 4 4+

Ex. 3.2 - C Major Scale to G

4+ 4 5+ 5 6+ 6 7 7+   8 8+ 9 9+ 9 8+ 8 7+   7 6 6+ 5 5+ 4 4+

Ex. 3.3 - G Mixolydian Scale

6+ 6 7 7+ 8 8+ 9 9+   9 8+ 8 7+ 7 6 6+

Ex. 3.4 - D Dorian Scale

4 5+ 5 6+ 6 7 7+ 8   7+ 7 6 6+ 5 5+ 4

Ex. 3.5 - C Major Four Pattern

4+ 4 5+ 4+ 4 5+ 5 4   5+ 5 6+ 5+ 5 6+ 6 5   6+ 6 7 6+ 6 7 7+ 6

7 7+ 8 7 7+ 8 8+ 7+   8 8+ 9 8 8+ 9 9+ 8+   9 9+ 10 9 10+

6

Ex. 3.6 - G Mixolydian Triplet Pattern

Ex. 3.7 - G Mixolydian One Step Back

Ex. 3.8 - G Mixolydian Swing Up

Dip Bend (Slight upward bend)

| 3 | 4 | 4 | 5+ | 6+ | 6+ | 7 | 8 | 8 | 8+ | 9+ | 9+ | 9 | 8 | 8 | 7 | 6+ | 6+ | 5 | 4 | 4 | 3 | 2 | 2 |

The next couple exercises focus on developing your double-tonguing and ability to make jumps. The articulation will be written below each hole number.

Ex. 3.9 - Double Tonguing

| 2 | 2 | 2 | 2 | 3 | 3 | 3 | 3 | 2 | 2 | 2 | 2 | 1 | 1 | 1 | 1 | 2 | 2 | 2 | 2 | 3 | 3 | 3 | 3 | 2 | 2 | 2 | 2 | 1 | 1 | 1 | 1 |
| Ta | Ka | Ta | Ka | Ta | Ka | Ta | Ka | Ta | Ka | Ta | Ka | Ta | Ka | Ta | Ka | Ta | Ka | Ta | Ka | Ta | Ka | Ta | Ka | Ta | Ka | Ta | Ka | Ta | Ka | Ta | Ka |

Ex. 3.10 - Double Tonguing with Jumps

| 2 | 2 | 2 | 2 | 3 | 2 | 2 | 2 | 4+ | 2 | 2 | 2 | 4 | 2 | 2 | 2 | 5+ | 2 | 2 | 2 | 5 | 2 | 2 | 2 | 6+ | 2 | 2 | 2 | 2 |
| Ta | Ka | Ta | Ka | Ta | Ha | Ta | Ka | Ha | Ka | Ta | Ka | Ta | Ka | Ta | Ka | Ha | Ka | Ta | Ka | Ha | Ka | Ta | Ka | Ha | Ka | Ta | Ka | Ta |

Section 4 – Bending Exercises

The first step in building bending proficiency is to play all of the chromatic tones available to you in tune. Play example 4.1 along with the recording to work on this. Exercises 4.2 through 4.17 will walk you through each level of bending proficiency. When moving from a bent note draw to an unbent note draw pay particular attention that the second note is not bent (exercises 4.7 though 4.11.)

Ex. 4.1 - Diatonic Harmonica Chromatic Scale

8va _ _ _ _ _ _ _ _ _ _ _ _ _

| 1+ | 1' | 1 | 2+ | 2" | 2' | 2 | 3'" | 3" | 3' | 3 | 4+ | 4' | 4 | 5+ | 5 | 6+ | 6' | 6 | 7 | 7+ | 8 | 8'+ | 8+ | 9 | 9'+ | 9+ | 10 | 10"+ | 10'+ | 10+ |
| C | Db | D | E | F | Gb | G | Ab | A | Bb | B | C | Db | D | E | F | G | Ab | A | Bb | C | D | Eb | E | F | Gb | G | A | Bb | B | C |

Ex. 4.2 - Bending for Expression

6   6'   6   4   4'   4   3   3"   3   2   2"   2   1   1'   1

Ex. 4.3

4   4'   4   5   3   3"   3   4   2   2"   2   3   1   1'   1   2

Ex. 4.4 - Stopping at the Bottom

6   6'   4   4'   3   3"   2   2"   1   1'

Ex. 4.5

6   6'   6   4   4'   4   3   3"   3   2   2"   2   1   1'   1

Ex. 4.6

6   6'   6+   4   4'   4+   3   3"   3+   2   2"   2+   1   1'   1+

Ex. 4.7 - Playing a Single Note After a Bend

6   6'   6   4   4'   4   3   3"   3   2   2"   2   1   1'   1

Ex. 4.8 - Starting at the Bottom

6 6'   6' 6   4 4'   4' 4   3 3"   3" 3   2 2"   2" 2   1 1'   1' 1

Ex. 4.9

Ex. 4.10

Ex. 4.11 - The Bent Turnaround

Ex. 4.12 - Bending for Expression (All notes are notated one octave lower than they sound)

Ex. 4.13 - Stopping at the Bottom

Ex. 4.14

Ex. 4.15 - Starting at the Bottom

Ex. 4.16

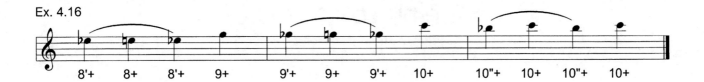

| 8'+ | 8+ | 8'+ | 9+ | 9'+ | 9+ | 9'+ | 10+ | 10"+ | 10+ | 10"+ | 10+ |

Ex. 4.17 - Bent Turnaround

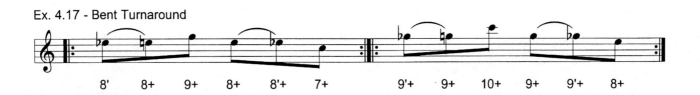

| 8' | 8+ | 9+ | 8+ | 8'+ | 7+ | 9'+ | 9+ | 10+ | 9+ | 9'+ | 8+ |

Section 5 – **Full Modes & Scales**

Detailed on the following pages are the modes (which we looked at earlier) in their entirety. The scales chosen for notation are based on the most commonly used or most usable scales within the first four positions of the harmonica. Positions are based on the key chart known as the Circle of Fifths. 1st Position uses the C scale for the I chord, the F scale for the IV chord, and the G scale for the V chord. 2nd Position uses the G scale for the I chord, the C scale for the IV chord, and the D scale for the V chord. 3rd Position uses the D scale for the I chord, the G scale for the IV chord, and the A scale for the V chord. 4th Position uses the A scale for the I chord, the D scale for the IV chord, and the E scale for the V chord. 4th Position is not used often but is used enough by players to warrant the scales to be in the book.

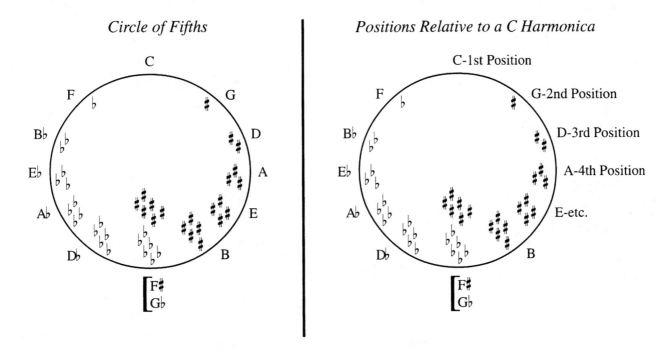

Circle of Fifths

Positions Relative to a C Harmonica

If a note is not available on the harmonica the note head will show as an "X" and there will be no tablature present for that note.

MAJOR DIATONIC SCALE
Major Diatonic Harmonica

DORIAN SCALE
Major Diatonic Harmonica

PHRYGIAN SCALE
Major Diatonic Harmonica

LYDIAN SCALE
Major Diatonic Harmonica

MIXOLYDIAN SCALE
Major Diatonic Harmonica

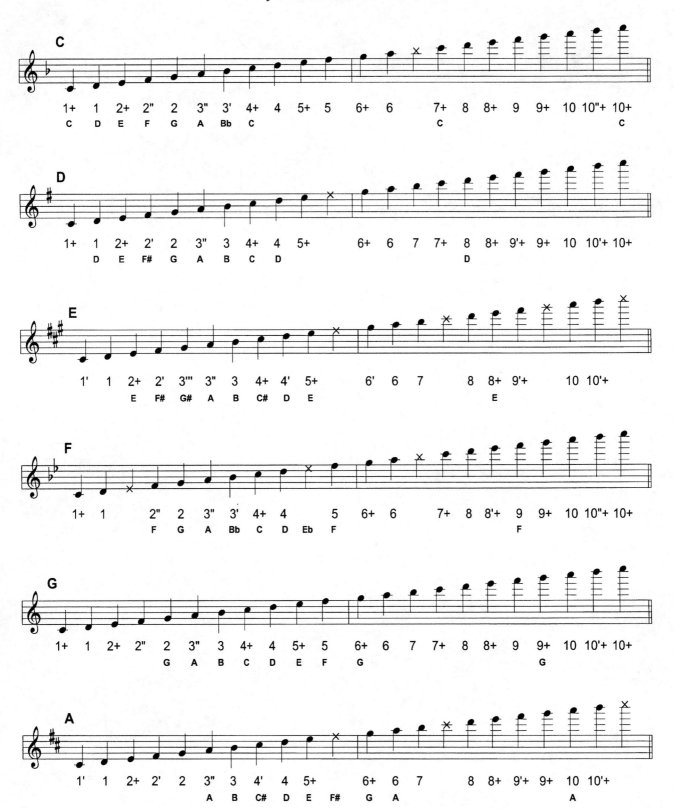

16

NATURAL MINOR & HARMONIC MINOR SCALE

Major Diatonic Harmonica

(3) = Indicates the note you raise for Harmonic Minor   (NA) = Not Available

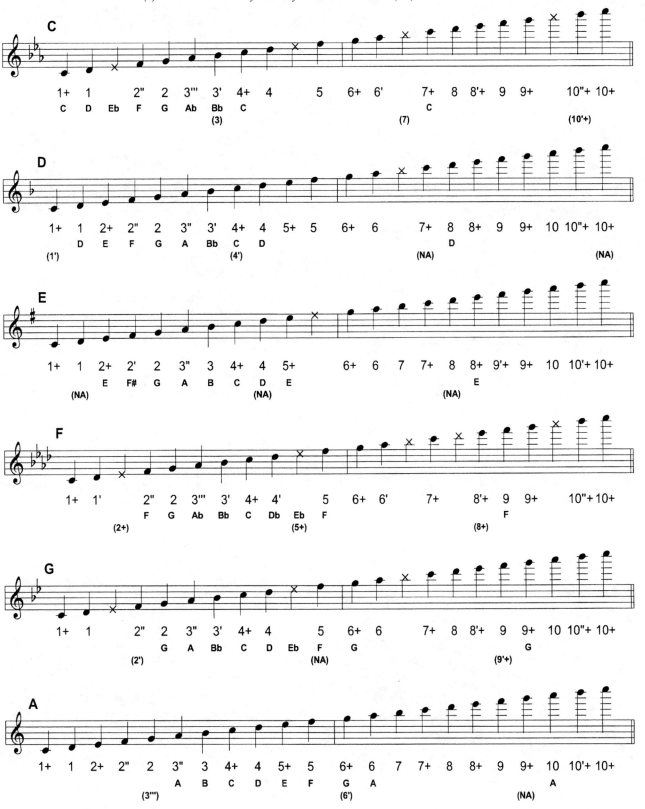

MAJOR PENTATONIC SCALE
Major Diatonic Harmonica

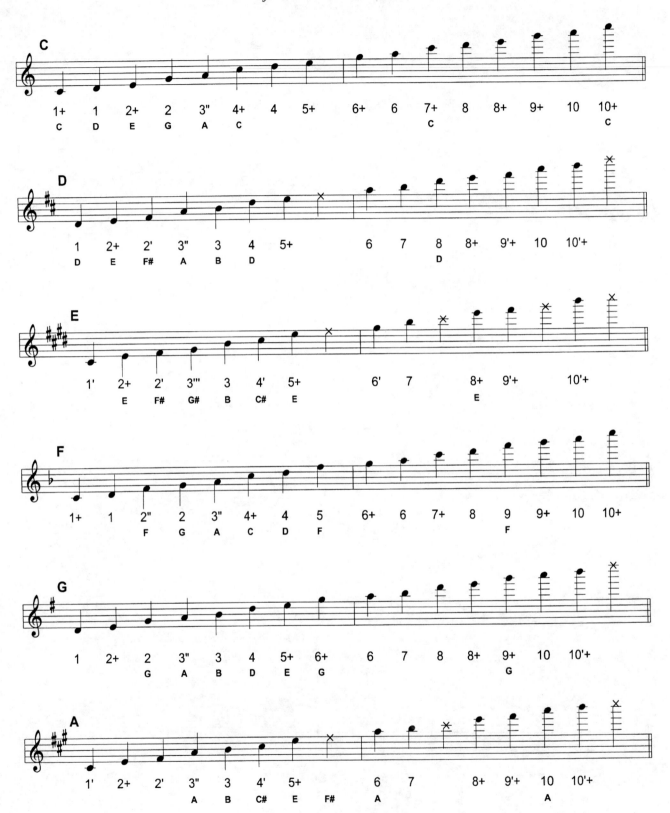

MINOR PENTATONIC SCALE
Major Diatonic Harmonica

C

1+   2"   2   3'   4+   5   6+   7+   8'+   9   9+   10"+   10+

C   Eb   F   G   Bb   C   C   C

D

1+   1   2"   2   3"   4+   4   5   6+   6   7+   8   9   9+   10   10+

D   F   G   A   C   D   D

E

1   2+   2   3"   3   4   5+   6+   6   7   8   8+   9+   10   10'+

E   G   A   B   D   E   E

F

1+   2"   3'"   3'   4+   5   6'   7+   8'+   9   10"+

F   Ab   Bb   C   Eb   F   F

G

1+   1   2"   2   3'   4+   4   5   6+   7+   8   9   9+   10"+   10+

G   Bb   C   D   F   G   G

A

1+   1   2+   2   3"   4+   4   5+   6+   6   7+   8   8+   9+   10   10+

A   C   D   E   G   A   A

19

BLUES SCALE
Major Diatonic Harmonica

WHOLE-TONE SCALE
Major Diatonic Harmonica

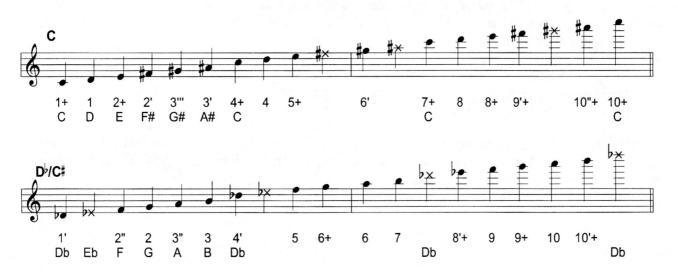

1+	1	2+	2'	3'''	3'	4+	4	5+	6'	7+	8	8+	9'+	10"+	10+
C	D	E	F#	G#	A#	C			C						C

1'	2"	2	3"	3	4'	5	6+	6	7	8'+	9	9+	10	10'+
Db	Eb	F	G	A	B	Db				Db				Db

CHROMATIC SCALE
Major Diatonic Harmonica

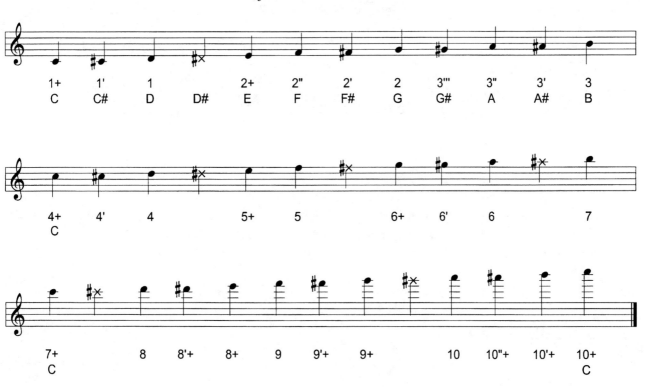

1+	1'	1	2+	2"	2'	2	3'''	3"	3'	3
C	C#	D	D#	E	F	F#	G	G#	A	A#	B

4+	4'	4	5+	5	6+	6'	6	7
C								

7+	8	8'+	8+	9	9'+	9+	10	10"+	10'+	10+
C										C

21

Section 6 – **Agility Exercises with Bends**

The most important scale available to you is the blues scale; knowing how to move across your harmonica fluidly using the blues scale is very important. Now that you have played all of the blues scales in their entirety, I want to give you some modified scales. These modified scales use bits of other blues scales to compensate for a weak section in a particular scale. The key to using combinations successfully is the use of the Elision. The ending of one scale is the beginning of the new scale; this is an elision. Look at how examples 6.1 and 6.2 have at least three notes that overlap in each scale; this creates a very strong transition between the scales.

The G blues scale has its weakness on the major 3rd on the 7th hole draw. The modified G blues scale uses a portion of the D blues scale from 8 draw to 4 draw to help make the G blues scale more bluesy. This is demonstrated below in example 6.1

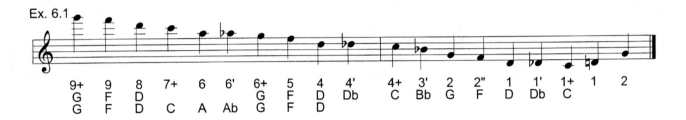

9+	9	8	7+	6	6'	6+	5	4	4'	4+	3'	2	2"	1	1'	1+	1	2
G	F	D		C	A	Ab	G	F	D	Db	Bb	G	F	D	Db	C		
G	F	D	C	A	Ab		G	F	D									

The C blues scale has its weakness in the middle octave from the 7th hole down to the 4th hole; there are no blue notes at all in this section. The modified C blues scale uses portions of the G and D blues scale in this range. This is demonstrated below in example 6.2.

10+	10"+	9+	9'+	9	8'+	8	7+	6	6'	6+	5	4	4'	4+	3'	2	2'	2"	2+	1+
C	Bb	G	Gb	F	Eb	-	C	A	Ab	G	F	D	Db	C	Bb	G	Gb	F	E	C
						D	C			G		F	D	Db	C	Bb	G			

The D blues scale is the most complete blues scale out of the three scales. The most difficult parts of this blues scale are the bends in the lower octave from the 4th hole down to the 1st hole. This modified D blues scale is more like a cool lick than a scale, but I think you'll like it. This is demonstrated below in example 6.3.

10	9+	9	8	7+	6	6'	6+	5	4	4	4+	3'''	3+	2	2"	1	1

All notes from D blues scale

Ex. 6.4 - C Chromatic Four Pattern

4+ 4' 4 4+ 4' 4 5+ 4' 4 5+ 5' 4 5+ 5' 5 5+ 5' 5 6+ 5' 5 6+ 6' 5 6+ 6' 6 6+ 6' 6 7 6'

6 7 7+ 6 7 7+ 8 7 7+ 8 8'+ 7+ 8 8'+ 8+ 8 8'+ 8+ 9 8'+ 8+ 9 9'+ 8+

9 9'+ 9+ 9 9'+ 9+ 10 9'+ 9+ 10 10"+ 9+ 10 10"+ 10'+ 10 10"+ 10'+ 10+ 10"+ 10+

Ex. 6.5 - G Chromatic Triplet Pattern

2+ 1+ 2+ 2" 1' 2" 2' 1' 2' 2 1 2 3''' 2+ 3''' 3" 2" 3" 3' 2' 3' 3 2 3

4+ 3+ 4+ 4' 3" 4' 4 3 4 5+ 4+ 5+ 5 4 5 6+ 5+ 6+ 6 5 6 7 6 7

7+ 6 7+ 8 7 8 8+ 7+ 8+ 9 8 9 9+ 9 8 7+ 6 6' 6+ 5 4 4' 4+ 3 2 2" 1 2

Ex. 6.6 - Lick Based Bending Exercise (2nd line is articulation, no mark indicates no articulation)

6 6' 6+ 5 5' 5+ 4 4' 4+ 3 3" 2 2 2" 1 3 2 2" 2
Too   Too   Too   Too   Da Too   Tee

Ex. 6.7 - Turn

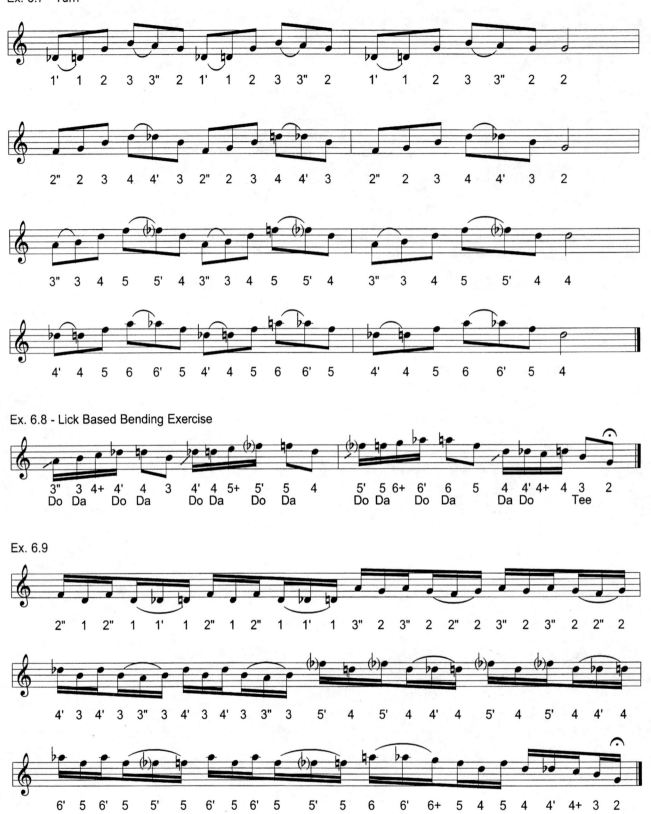

Ex. 6.8 - Lick Based Bending Exercise

Ex. 6.9